HODDER'S YE...
for the NATIONAL

A special introduction by Bill Corbett
for *Hodder's June Story Book*

Hamish
Climbing
Father's Mountain

My brother John had library tickets. I read all the books he bought home
but I envied him. One day he took me to the library. He whispered a few
words and then grinned and lifted me level with the counter.
'If he can write his name and address then he can join' smiled the lady.
I scrawled my practised signature and hoped. After peering she smiled
again and went ... 'stamp ... stamp ...'
From six years old till now that magic moment has never dimmed ...
For I'm a member of the library with a card to prove it.

A true story.

Hodder
Children's
Books

a division of Hodder Headline plc

*Also by WJ Corbett
for older readers*

The Dragon's Egg and Other Stories
The Battle of Chinnbrook Wood
The Ark of the People

Hamish
Climbing
Father's Mountain

by

W.J. CORBETT

Illustrated by
SUSAN HELLARD

Hodder
Children's
Books

a division of Hodder Headline plc

A Catalogue record for this book is available from the British Library

ISBN 0340 75275 0

Typeset by Avon Dataset Ltd, Bidford-on-Avon

Printed and bound in Great Britain by
The Guernsey Press Co. Ltd, Guernsey, Channel Islands

Hodder Children's Books
A Division of Hodder Headline plc
338 Euston Road
London NW1 3BH

For Sophie, Sam and Luke

CHAPTER ONE

"Hamish . . . oh Hamish . . . the winds have driven the clouds away, it's a perfect day for climbing . . ."

The taunt drifted down the rocky hillside and into the twitching ears of a small mountain goat.

Hamish hated voices interrupting his dreams. For in those dreams he could be the hero he was not in real life. It was bad enough having to endure the voices of his parents constantly nagging in his ears. Sighing, he turned over on his soft heathery bed on the valley floor and tried to fall back to sleep. But the voice of his enemy Haggis would not let him rest. Again the taunt came wafting down the hillside.

"Leave me alone when I'm not well," cried Hamish angrily. "I've woken up with a throbbing hoof this morning. How can I clatter up Father's Mountain with a handicapped hoof dragging behind me?"

It was a lie of course. But the lie came as no surprise to the climbing party of young goats clattering about high on the hillside. For it was well-known that Hamish was the biggest liar in the world.

In fact, Hamish had woken up with four perfectly sound hooves. His reason for lying was simple. Hamish the dreamer hated climbing mountains with every fibre of his being. And the gang of young goats giggling and nudging each other on the hillside knew this very well. Which was why they so enjoyed to hear Haggis bait the fiery Hamish. Meanwhile, Hamish snuggled his wispy beard deeper into his heathery bed on the safe valley floor and tried to blot out Haggis's sneers. But it was hard, for young goats have marvellous hearing.

"Hamish . . . oh Hamish . . . come with us, climb Father's Mountain almost to the very top," baited Haggis. "We are planning an assault on the lowest peak this beautiful climbing morning. Don't fob us off with more of your lies, Hamish. Surely you are not afraid to join us in our attempt to conquer that killer climb?"

"Stop pestering me when I'm not fit," Hamish yelled back. "I'll climb Father's Mountain when I'm good and ready. But on my own, and by night, probably. Anyway, it might be a nice morning right now, but I reckon it's going to storm later."

More lies of course. The thought of Hamish daring to set a hoof on Father's Mountain in broad daylight was incredible enough. But boasting that he intended to climb it alone and by moonlight was an even bigger joke. And as for his storm-warning, it was obvious to the gang on the hillside that the skies had never been bluer, the sun cheerier, nor the summer winds softer. It would have been a miracle had a single rain drop dared to blemish the perfection of that climbing morning. Just imagining Hamish being right sent the young goats into another fit of giggles. As for Hamish, he began to snore very loudly in the hope that this might fool his head into falling back to sleep. But the ruse didn't work, for small goats are extremely alert when they don't want to be.

"Hamish . . . oh Hamish . . . why don't you admit that you are just a cowardly liar?" called Haggis, his voice filled with scorn. "Why not come clean and admit that you fear to climb Father's Mountain because of what happened up there before you became a full-time orphan?"

The brutal words pierced Hamish's heart like knives. Squeezing shut his sad pink eyes he sobbed quietly to himself there on his heathery bed on the safe valley floor. He was remembering a time when he was a bit younger than now . . . a terrible day when a climbing party of grown-up goats came clattering down from the highest mountain to break some awful news to Hamish's mother who was busy cropping tasty nettles for tea.

"Hug Hamish tight," they warned her. "For we have clattered post-haste down the mountain to shatter his young life with the sad tidings that his father – your husband – has just plunged to his death from the highest peak in the Highlands, while showing-off before his many lady-friends. As this is the first bit of bad news Hamish has heard in his young life he might go into shock through grief. If he

Hamish

does we suggest you duck his head in an icy stream to bring him round. Incidentally, if you should also come over all faint we recommend that you duck your own head at the same time. But cures aside, back to the tragedy. Needless to say, we are all deeply sorry about this," and off they clattered for tea, nodding their thick beards in agreement that Hamish's flashy and charming father had had it coming to him for a long time. A while later they were piously naming the climb that Hamish's father had plummeted from, 'Father's Mountain'. "As a loving tribute," they said. Others believed that it was from plain, jealous spite on their part.

CHAPTER TWO

Hamish's weepy mother soon tired of ducking her unconscious son in icy streams. After a few days of having to prepare tea for them both without father's help, for he had always brought down from the mountains a sprig of herbs to brighten their meal, she soon turned dry-eyed and bitter. She took to ordering small, knock-kneed and trembling Hamish to stand before her so that she could lash him with her sharp tongue.

"So, how does it feel to know that your adored father was nothing but a flashy, nimble-hoofed charmer?" she snapped. Then her eyes would flash with an unholy and savage light, "though he wasn't so charming and nimble when he plunged to his death while showing-off before his many lady-friends, was he? So, Hamish my lad, let his death be a lesson to you. If you also have ambitions of growing up to become a lady-chasing Romeo, forget it. I'm saying this because I've noticed how happy and mischievous you can be when you aren't falling down unconscious with grief. Remember, Hamish, I'm warning you for your own good. Settle down to some sober and serious living or one day you'll be the next goat who won't come clattering home for tea."

From that day forth Hamish became a very boring little goat indeed. Never again did he prank and play with his mischievous friends. Never again did he beat them in races up the lower slopes of the mountains, though he could have done, he being a gifted climber like his late father. For the thought of growing up a smooth show-off like his father frightened him to death. Even when his dry-eyed and bitter mother passed away unexpectedly, still he refused to take up his once mischievous life. The only comfort he got from the death of his mother was that never once did he fall down unconscious when thinking about her memory. But he never broke free from her influence. For as he grew up alone, a full-time orphan, again and again her ghostly voice from Heaven hammered and nagged away in his left ear, advising him to always clatter the path of goodness.

"Remember to stay sober and serious, son," she warned. "Steer clear of all things flashy and charming. For you don't want to end up never coming home for tea like you-know-who, do you?"

Not to be outdone, the spirit of his father had taken up residence in Hamish's right ear. His father's ghost was more jovial and said things like, "what's wrong with being a bit flashy, son? Why make yourself miserable trying to live a life as-good-as-gold? Remember, Hamish, we only have one bite at that succulent cherry called life. So go out and sink your teeth in it while you can."

But because of his parents' constant nagging in his ears there weren't many cherries in life for a small mountain goat called Hamish. Torn between their nagging in his ears he attempted to enjoy life in the only way left to him. Hamish became a dreamer. He soon found out that dreaming was almost as real as life if one put one's mind to it. He also found out that dreams almost came true if practised a lot. Like being a hero, for instance. Suddenly the sneering voice of Haggis was shocking him back from his dreams to the here and now of a perfect climbing morning.

"Why don't you throw off that quite good, bad hoof and clatter up the hillside to join our climbing-party, Hamish?" Haggis called teasingly down. Then he delivered the shot that he knew his rival would bristle at. "Did you know Hannah is climbing with us this morning? She isn't afraid to climb Father's Mountain. Or don't you care that she must think you a coward?"

That did it. The thought that Hannah might think badly of him roused Hamish to a fury. Scrambling to his hooves he threw back his wispy beard to bellow up the hill. "Hannah would never think me a coward," he cried. "She knows that if my hoof was fit I would eagerly clatter up the hillside and lead the climbing party up Father's Mountain, don't you, Hannah?"

"If only I could believe you, Hamish," cried Hannah, all distressed. "But you keep telling so many wicked lies all the time. If only you weren't such a dreamer, and would come out and live life as it should be lived. If only you would stand up and be your own goat, Hamish."

"But I am standing up, Hannah," called Hamish desperately. "I am my own goat, would I ever lie to you?"

"But it's the way you are standing that bothers me, Hamish," cried Hannah forlornly, "for if you had a bad hoof, surely it would be cocked-up beneath you in pain? Yet from here it appears that you are standing firmly on all four of them. And there is also the weather-forecast prediction, Hamish. How can it possibly storm on such a perfect climbing morning as this? Yet, Hamish, your cowardly lies aside, I still believe that deep down you belong amongst the bravest of the brave."

"But never bravely flashy, Hannah,"

called back Hamish, fearfully. "For I'm convinced that Haggis is much flashier and more charming than me. I just hope for his sake that he arrives back from the mountains in time for tea. I may not like him, but I wouldn't wish him harm."

"I've never arrived home late for tea yet," sneered Haggis. "So what will you be doing while the rest of us are conquering the first peak of Father's Mountain? Lying on your heathery bed, dreaming your life away, as usual?"

"Hamish most certainly will not," cried Hannah sharply. She was gazing anxiously down at Hamish who was gazing anxiously up, one hoof now cocked painfully up beneath him. "I am willing to bet that after we've gone Hamish will leap from his bed and do something exciting and dangerous. Like a new hobby until his hoof gets better and his weather-forecasting improves. Isn't that so, Hamish?"

"Exactly so, Hannah," shouted

16

Hamish, thinking furiously. Then a brilliant idea came to him. "As a matter of fact, while you lot are sheltering from the fierce storm up the mountain, I will be practising a new hobby that will put Haggis in the shade."

"And what new hobby is that, you little liar?" scoffed Haggis, jealous of Hannah's defence of his rival. "How about chaffinch-spotting? Now there's a nice gentle hobby for a goat who is too afraid to climb his own father's mountain."

"That's just where you're wrong, Haggis," yelled Hamish furiously. "In fact my new hobby is twice as dangerous as chaffinch-spotting. It's called pot-holing. I intend to take up underground exploring and will probably end up discovering the centre of the earth."

Yet another obvious lie was too much for the gang of young goats on the hillside. They laughed so much that some of them slipped from the boulders they were balanced on, painfully bumping their bearded chins on the stony slope.

"Who ever heard of a pot-holing mountain goat?" shouted Haggis, roaring with laughter. "How can the wind dash through one's beard in the still underground? Enough of your lies, Hamish, we have lost patience with you and your silly talk. Come gang, let's leave the poor soul to his dreaming, for the living challenge of Father's Mountain is calling us upwards." So saying he leapt from the needle-sharp rock he was poised on and clattered off up the hillside, the gang of eager young goats hard on his heels. Only Hannah hesitated.

"Goodbye, Hamish," she called down softly. "Enjoy your pot-holing. But really go, for you won't let me down, will you? And then when we return from Father's Mountain you will be able to thrill us with tales of life underground. For always remember, Hamish, I will ever have faith in your deep-down bravery, even if I am the only goat who has." Then she too was gone.

As the clatter and the happy chatter of the climbing-party died away up the hillside so Hamish slumped down on his heathery bed safe on the valley floor and wept more splashy tears into his wispy beard. Not even the song of a neighbouring lark, joyously climbing to Heaven, could rouse him from his bleak despair. For it seemed to Hamish that even that small friend was mocking him.

"I will go pot-holing, I won't be put off," whispered Hamish fiercely. "I'll prove to Hannah that I'm no coward."

"That's my son," encouraged the ghostly voice of his father in his right ear. "Go out and snatch at life. Take risks and be admired for it. For what's wrong with a mountain goat strutting his stuff if he has the stuff to strut?"

"Strut at your peril, Hamish," hissed mother's spirit in his left ear. "Trot gently through life with your head bowed low to hide the gorgeous looks you inherited from your rascally father. For his perfect profile did him no good when his hooves slipped off the mountain, did it?" Pulled this way and that by the voices in his head Hamish tried to shut them out by retreating into his safe world of harmless dreams. But that day he found no peace there. Only nightmares which seemed very, very real . . .

. . . he could hear Hannah's desperate cries for help as she lay trapped in the dark pot-hole underground.

"Help me, Hamish," she screamed. "I can't move, and I'm being eaten alive by hordes of little blind snapping crabs."

"There's nothing I can do, Hannah," Hamish shouted back, fearful of venturing beyond the entrance to the pot-hole. "My handicapped hoof is not fit enough to dash inside and rescue you. And not only that, but after the terrible storm we've had the waters are cascading down the mountain and will soon flood out the pot-hole. If I limped inside then both of us would be eaten alive and also drowned."

Just then Haggis came clattering down the hillside. Roughly shoving Hamish aside he disappeared into the pot-hole, worming and scrambling along the rapidly flooding passages to where Hannah lay trapped so helplessly. Some time later he emerged dragging a weeping and choking Hannah behind

him. Though fearfully nipped by crabs and half-drowned, Haggis still managed to look the perfect picture of a hero. A chorus of cheers arose from the gang of anxiously waiting goats. Haggis had attempted the impossible and had pulled it off. Alone and ignored, Hamish hung his head in shame as the hero and his heroine were clattered off to enjoy a slap-up tea in celebration.

Hamish awoke with a heart-thumping start. Through bleary eyes he saw that the sun was beginning to sink behind the mountains. A contented 'cheep' from just beyond the tip of his wispy beard told him that his neighbouring lark had returned from his trip to Heaven's Gate, his throat hoarse from all his 'Hallelujahing'. And Hamish was filled with self-loathing as the memories of that terrible nightmare came drifting back to him.

"Cringing worm," muttered the ghost

of his father in his right ear. "To think that a son of mine could dream such cowardly dreams. If only I had bred a son like Haggis." "Take no notice, Hamish," whispered his mother in his left ear. "Never mind what folk call you, son. Leave the flashy rescuing to those goats who are bound to come to a sticky end. I refer to that same Haggis who will one day never make it home for tea."

But Haggis did. And so did the gang, plus Hannah. Poised on the hillside overlooking Hamish's heathery bed they looked extremely wind-swept and healthy as they gazed down on the poor wretch that was Hamish. Haggis was in a crowing mood.

"Hamish, oh Hamish, guess who's just conquered the lower peak of Father's Mountain?" he boasted. "Of course, being a 'ladies always first' goat, I naturally insisted that Hannah should have the honour of being the first to step on to that frightening peak. But it was I who blazed the trail to the summit. So how went your chaffinch spotting . . . sorry, I meant pot-holing? I must say you don't look very muddy and wet to me. But then, I wouldn't be surprised to learn that you hadn't stirred from your heathery bed for one second of this perfect climbing day."

"Perhaps Hamish explored a clean pot-hole and arrived home early for tea?" defended Hannah, hoping with all her heart that this was so. "Could that be true, Hamish?"

"You are spot on, Hannah," called Hamish, yet another lie tripping easily off his tongue. "For we expert pot-holers learn to avoid the muddy tunnels in the deep and dangerous underground. As you say, we like to get home clean and early for tea."

"So, what happened to the famous storm, then?" sneered Haggis, annoyed that Hannah would defend such a wimp as Hamish. "I suppose it disappeared in the same puff of smoke as your so-called handicapped hoof did? So, brave underground explorer, when do you think you will be fit enough to do some real goat's work like climbing Father's Mountain with the rest of us? Maybe . . . sometime . . . perhaps . . . or never . . . ?"

"Sooner than you think, Haggis," shouted Hamish, angrily. "When I'm properly fit I will show you some real climbing. Not only up one peak at a time, but straight up to the very top one."

"Sounds like dream-climbing to me," mocked Haggis. Then suddenly he tired of baiting his rival. "Oh, come on gang, let's leave the little liar in his Land of Nod. I for one am starving for my tea. My mum says it's sour goosegogs and nettles tonight . . . lovely nosh," and off he clattered along the perilous ridge to where his parents lived, his tongue licking at his chops in anticipation, the gang hard on his heels eagerly licking theirs. Only Hannah remained on the hillside looking down at Hamish's lonely bed on the safe valley floor.

"I'm also going for my tea now, Hamish," she called softly. "But I hope to see you fit and well, come the next perfect climbing morning. For then you won't need to go pot-holing – which you never did anyway. So please, Hamish, snap out of your dream world and stop dwelling on the awful past since you became an orphan. Try to stand tall and be your own goat for once. For I know you have it in you. And always remember, Hamish, I will ever believe that deep down you belong amongst the bravest of the brave." And then she too was gone, her hunger for tea over-ruling her kind heart. For that night, her mother had promised, Hannah would enjoy her favourite dish of bright-red, squashy elderberries. And not even a goat with a heart as kind as Hannah's could resist that tempting fare.

Alone again and filled with self-hatred and despair, Hamish slumped down on his heathery bed and wept more tears from his pink eyes. His grief was terrible. On top of that were the nagging voices of his parents who continued to shout advice in both his ears. And as Hamish tried to sleep so he vowed many things. He vowed that, for the love of Hannah, the morning would greet a new Hamish. A Hamish able to stand on his own four hooves. A Hamish ready to face the real world and all it could hurl at him. A Hamish who would arise and put the flashy Haggis in his place. For some time Hamish gazed at the moon, his pink eyes a-glow with determination. Then he slept, his dreams filled with deeds of rescuing Hannah from all kinds of perils, the hours till dawn only disturbed by the cheerful piping of the neighbouring larks.

CHAPTER THREE

"Hamish, oh Hamish, the weather looks set fair again, it's time for some more climbing . . ."

The challenge floated down the hillside and into the cringing ears of a small mountain goat.

Grumbling softly, Hamish turned over on his heathery bed and tried to blank out the hateful voice of his rival. But it was difficult, for young goats are extremely sensitive to the voices of other goats who don't like them. Again the jibe came down the hillside causing Hamish to flare with anger as he always did.

"Leave me alone when I'm poorly," he yelled back. "I've woken up with a head like a turnip this morning. How can I clatter up Father's Mountain when my head feels as heavy as a huge turnip?"

It was a huge lie of course. It seemed that Hamish's vows of the previous night had come to nothing. For he had woken up with his head feeling nothing like a huge turnip. Rather, as usual, it felt as light as a lettuce. His reason for lying was simple. He was still afraid of climbing Father's Mountain, down to the tiniest fibre of his small being. The gang of young goats giggling and nudging each other high on the hillside weren't surprised. They expected Hamish the coward to make excuses. Which why they egged Haggis on to further bait the silly Hamish. Meanwhile, Hamish nuzzled his wispy beard into the nest of his neighbouring sky-lark, for the happy cheeping of that complete family always comforted him. But the parent birds had other ideas. They wanted nothing to do with the coward next-door. Especially when they had three impressionable chicks to rear. At once the father lark ordered a nest-move to a hummock of turf a bit further away, pecking Hamish sharply on the nose as a punishment before moving into his new home.

"Hamish, oh Hamish, this glorious morning is made just for goats who have the guts to clatter up dangerous mountains," taunted Haggis. "So where are your guts, turnip head? Aren't you envious that we, the gang, are determined to wear the second peak of Father's Mountain as a feather in our caps before tea-time tonight?"

"Stop bothering me when my head is out of condition," raged Hamish up the hillside. "I will climb Father's Mountain when it's as light as a lettuce again. But on my own, and when the sky is black and full of shrieking bats, probably. Anyway, the morning might be calm now, but I reckon we're in for a hurricane later."

Was there no end to Hamish's lies, the gang on the hillside marvelled? Did he really expect them to believe that he would brave Father's Mountain on a bat-black night when he wouldn't even tackle it in bright sunshine? And as for his hurricane theory, weren't the breezes now wafting over their Highland home as light as thistledown, or a lettuce even? Trying to imagine Hamish's hurricane whirling them into the air made them collapse in giggling heaps, some of them cracking their shins on the razor-sharp rocks that rolled from beneath them without warning. As for Hamish, he tried to ignore their mockery by plumping up his heathery bed and praying for a pleasant dream to engulf him. But the dream wouldn't come, for young mountain goats get very restless when they are laughed at two days running.

"What a pity your turnip head won't allow you to come, Hamish," mocked Haggis. "Especially when Hannah is climbing with us again. I expect she thinks you the most cowardly goat in the world for being afraid to set hoof where your own father once trod."

The truth in those spiteful words brought tears to Hamish's pink eyes again. At once Hannah was leaping to his defence.

"Can Hamish help his head feeling like a turnip?" she cried, spinning around on her boulder to face the bullying Haggis. "But he won't always be ill. I'm willing to bet when he's properly fit he will take up his rightful place at the head of our climbing-party and lead us higher and higher up Father's Mountain, won't you, Hamish?"

"You are always right, Hannah," shouted Hamish, drying his eyes with the tip of his wispy beard. "Then I'll show Haggis how bravely I can climb."

"But not today, eh, Hamish?" replied Haggis, spitefully. "So what will you be doing while we are conquering the second peak of Father's Mountain? Lying on your heathery bed wrapped in dreams as usual? Like yesterday when you expected us to believe that you were exploring bone-dry pot-holes deep underground?"

"I'm sure that Hamish has some new hobby in the planning stage, am I right, Hamish?" called Hannah down the hillside.

"When were you last wrong, Hannah?" cried Hamish, his brain thinking furiously. Suddenly he thought of a lie equally as absurd and as silly as yesterday's. "As a matter of fact I have decided to take up the dangerous hobby of long-distance swimming. I plan to count how many times I can goat-paddle up and down The Deep Loch that lies at the bottom of The Great Glacier. And if the scaly monster who lives there rises to the top and tries to swallow me down for lunch, I'll kick him on the nose with my sharp hoof."

"Who ever heard of a long distance swimming mountain goat?" chortled Haggis. "Goats are born to strike sparks from rocks, not paddle with hooves under water? Pull my other hoof, Hamish, it's got bells on."

The gang of goats balanced on their rocks high on the hillside also thought that Hamish's new hobby was the looniest yet. If like Haggis they had had bells on their hooves they would have rung them cheerfully. But as they hadn't they contented themselves with falling about with laughter, some of them again painfully bumping their beardy chins on the hard slope.

"Well, I think the new hobby is the bravest ever," cried Hannah, pretending to shudder. "In fact it sounds so perilous that I wish someone would try to stop him. But then, if Hamish is determined to set a new swimming-record while being half-swallowed by the great monster, who are we ordinary goats to try to stop him. But I really do feel that Hamish is being a little over-valiant this time."

"Over-valiant, but never flashy, eh, Hannah?" shouted Hamish anxiously. "For I am determined to live my life as

modestly as possible. It has never been my aim to be a show-off like Haggis."

"Well, I think your new hobby is piffle," scoffed Haggis. "What's the betting that as soon as we turn our backs you will be snoring on your heathery bed again? Oh, come on gang, don't let's waste any more words on him. For we have the second peak of Father's Mountain to conquer on this superb climbing morning." So saying he turned a contemptuous rump to the upwardly glaring Hamish, leapt from his needle-sharp rock, and began to clatter up the hillside, the excited and high-jumping gang in hot pursuit. Only Hannah remained behind.

"Good luck with your goat-paddling in The Loch, Hamish," she called softly down. "And if the monster proves too fierce to tackle, promise me that you will swim for the shore at once. And Hamish, I really do hope that you are sincere about your hobby this time. Only you do tend to tell lies and let me down a great deal. So this time buckle to it Hamish. Then when we return from the mountains you can regale us with horror stories about deep black whirlpools and ravenous monsters that will make our beards curl. And Hamish, always remember that in spite of all I still have faith in your deep-down bravery."

Then she too turned and clattered off up the hillside.

CHAPTER FOUR

Alone with his misery and empty lies again, Hamish slumped down on his heathery bed and tried to close his ears to the voices of his dead parents who were bickering in his head as usual. From their new nest two hummocks of turf away the lark family eyed him stonily. They had no time for young goats who lay around blubbing while the rest of the world got on with the job of worshipping God, and doing their best, however hard the road might be. Casting Hamish one last hard look the lark took to the sky, his chicks envying his skill.

"I will go swimming in the Loch, I will kick the monster on the nose," vowed Hamish suddenly rousing himself. "This time I won't let Hannah down."

"Now you're talking, son," said the pleased voice of his father in his right ear. "Get down to the Loch and swank a bit. Sure it's risky, but isn't simply poking one hoof out of bed each morning a risk – for life is risk, son."

"And what if Hamish dives in The Loch and discovers he can't swim?" hissed mother, fiercely. "And what if the monster croaks 'phooey' when Hamish tries to kick him on the nose? Listen to me, Hamish, leave those dare-devil tricks to the likes of that Haggis who's going to miss out on his tea one day."

His head reeling from that royal battle going on inside his head, Hamish tried to blot it out in the only way he knew. But once again the cosy dream he sought swiftly became a nightmare . . .

. . . the fury of the hurricane blasting down the slopes of the Great Glacier whipped the surface of the Loch into huge pounding waves. Bobbing amongst those waves, Hamish heard the hysterical voice of Hannah as she tried to keep her bearded chin above water.

"I am about to go down for the second time, Hamish," she gurgled, her hooves clawing desperately at a small floating straw. "I'm afraid I'm too exhausted to make the shore alone. Save yourself, Hamish, for I'd hate to think that you will also drown performing an unselfish act."

"Very well, Hannah," yelled Hamish, turning and striking for the shore. "For what with the hurricane and the giant waves, I couldn't possibly save us both."

"Out of the way, turnip-head,"

spluttered a harsh voice that caused Hamish's faint heart to sink. It was Haggis. Hooves windmilling flashily, he swam past his rival to where Hannah was just about to go down for the third and final time.

To mighty cheers from the watching goats, Haggis came surfing into the shore on a boiling wave, strongly towing a sopping wet Hannah. Alone and out of it, the cowardly and shivering Hamish looked on in shame. He was not invited to the party thrown in honour of brave Haggis, the saviour of the adorable Hannah.

With a fearful yell Hamish awoke. Through heavy pink eyes he saw the sun about to set beyond the mountains. From nearby he heard some sleepy "clucks". The lark, yet another crack at Heaven abandoned for the day, was back with his family, one Heaven at least assured, the Heaven of his family.

Suddenly, snatches of that awful night-mare began to filter back into Hamish's fevered brain. And he was filled with bitterness. For even his dreams, his escape from reality, betrayed him now . . .

"You pathetic excuse for a son," shouted the wrathful voice of his father in his right ear. "If my sharp left hoof wasn't roasting in Hell I would clip your left ear."

"And if my sharp left hoof wasn't in Heaven I would pat our Hamish on his right one," said mother smugly in her son's left ear. "For I think he behaved very sensibly to escape from the monster and The Loch by leaving the flashy rescuing to that Haggis. Now there's a show-off goat who won't always be so lucky."

But for that day at least, Haggis was lucky. So was the rest of the climbing party including Hannah. For all at once they were there on the hillside, clattering about and chattering amongst themselves about the exciting events of the day. Haggis was in a boastful mood again.

"Hamish, oh Hamish, guess who's wearing the second peak of Father's Mountain as a feather in his cap?" he shouted down. "Of course, being a well-mannered goat I stood aside to allow Hannah the honour of stepping onto it first, but it was I who urged the party upwards when the going got tough. So how went your swimming in The Loch then? Did you set a record for we mountain goats who never go near water? So when do you plan to break it, for *we* will never want to? And did you get to kick the monster on the nose? I must say, you don't look like you've been near water to me. You look as dry as a bone from up here."

"Hamish could easily have dried off in the hot sun before we returned," flared Hannah, protectively. "Is there any truth in what I'm saying, Hamish?"

"You always tell the truth, Hannah,"

lied Hamish at the top of his voice.
"Haggis will no doubt gulp to learn that I
swam the Loch one hundred times there
and back, and twice kicked the monster
in the mouth."

"What, and all in a hurricane-force
wind?" mocked Haggis. "By the way,
what happened to your hurricane? For
the gang will tell you that the air was as
smooth as silk up on Father's Mountain.
But then you wouldn't care, you being
so afraid to go near it. Unless you can
summon up the nerve on the next
perfect climbing morning?"

"You try to stop me, Haggis,"
bellowed Hamish, his pink eyes flashing
anger. "For my head won't always feel
like a turnip. When it heals I will be
showing you a clean pair of heels up the
mountain."

"That'll be the day," Haggis sneered.
Then, tiring of making his rival look
small, said "Okay, gang, let's scatter
home for tea. Let's leave poor Hamish to

his dreams, for I expect he's anxious to return to them. Anyway, I'm ravenous, and it's fresh spiky thistles tonight, smashing scoff," and off he clattered drooling into his wispy beard, the gang bounding along behind drooling as well. Only Hannah remained, even though she was drooling with hunger herself.

"You've let me down, haven't you, Hamish?" she called sadly. "You haven't been swimming in the Loch or fighting the monster at all. In fact you haven't stirred all day from your heathery bed, have you? Well, Hamish, before I also dash off home for my tea, remember I won't always stick up for you if you don't change your ways. I'm warning you, if tomorrow's dawn doesn't usher in a new Hamish it will be the finish between us. So for Heaven's sake shrug off your hang-ups, Hamish, and try to remember that I desperately want to believe in your deep-down bravery." Then she too clattered off along the narrow track that lead to home, her hungry mouth watering into her wispy beard. She didn't look back as she usually did.

It was another night of wretched soul-searching for the lonely Hamish. But not a quiet one. For what with the ghost of his mother hissing advice in his left ear, and the spirit of his father shouting "ignore the old nag" in his right, Hamish felt that his head was going to split right open. And then, there was Hannah's warning to worry about. Hamish knew that if she finally lost all faith in him he would be finished, totally. Which all at once fired him up yet again.

"This worm is determined to turn," he shouted at the Highland sky. "I will become the old Hamish I used to be, and make Hannah proud of me. I will . . . I will . . ."

The moved-away lark also had worms on his mind. He was dreaming about a whole banquet of them, enough to feed his whole family come the dawn. But in his dream he did spare a thought for his miserable ex-neighbour. For though the little bird was thoroughly disgusted by

Hamish's cowardliness, he still, like Hannah, held a soft spot in his heart for the mixed-up goat. And so, as he dreamed his dream about lovely worms, he spared a spot in his dream for one particular worm. A worm that he also desperately hoped would turn. A little goat called Hamish . . .

CHAPTER FIVE

"Hamish, oh Hamish, the sun is toiling up the sky, we too are going climbing," the mocking voice came drifting down the hillside and into the fed-up ears of a small mountain goat.

Hamish lay still and pretended to be dead. But the ploy didn't work, for the chests of young mountain goats heave like bellows when they are distressed. The lark who had been tugging worms since first light was outraged. Obviously, the four-hoofed worm he had been rooting for in his dream was not for turning. At once the tiny bird ordered his family to again move home, to a clump of turf even further away from the despicable Hamish. Then, spreading his wings he leapt into the sky, anxious to have another crack at Heaven. Meanwhile, Hamish was scrambling to his feet, yet another excuse babbling from his mouth.

"Leave me alone when I've woken up sick for the third morning in a row," he raged up the hillside. "Can I help it if I've woken up with double-vision in both eyes? How can I lead you all up Father's Mountain when I can see four of everything?"

It was a stupendous whopper of a lie, of course. For Hamish had woken up with his pink eyes as keen as mustard. The reason for the lie was simple. Despite all his soul-searching and vows of the night before, he was as afraid of climbing Father's Mountain today as any day. The gang of goats on the hillside were filled with scorn, but with admiration too. For without doubt, Hamish just had to be the most superb and exciting liar the Highlands had ever known. Eyes rolling in wonder, they waited for Haggis to slay Hamish with a devastating put-down. In the meantime Hamish was trying to prove that his eye-sight problem was genuine by deliberately stumbling into hummocks of turf in an attempt to trip himself over. The lady-lark who was guarding the new nest and her three new chicks heaved a sigh of relief. Thank Heaven her husband had ordered another, safer nest move only just in time.

"Hamish, oh Hamish, stop acting the giddy goat," sang Haggis, gleefully. "No goat ever woke up three mornings in a row with three different types of illness. Why not come out with it and admit in

Hannah's hearing that you are simply a cowardly worm who will never turn. Then we will finally leave you alone to stew in your own thick Highland broth, won't we, Hannah?"

"I must say, I'm sorely tempted to leave Hamish to stew, Haggis," cried Hannah, her mauve eyes flashing down the hill at the silly sight of Hamish falling on his nose. "For I'm coming to the conclusion that a certain goat is beyond help. Do you hear me, Hamish? Do you realise that your last chance to make good is slipping away?"

"I can hear you loud and clear, Hannah," shouted Hamish, slipping on his nose again. "But the problem is I'm having difficulty seeing you on account of my double vision. Tell me, are you the pretty goat on the left or the attractive goat on the right, or are you one of the two gorgeous ones in the middle?"

"That does it, Hamish," shouted Hannah, fuming. "Stay in your world of lies and dreams. I'm through with you, do you hear me?"

"Hearing isn't my problem, Hannah," cried Hamish. "Ever since the death of my parents my ears have been filled with the sound of their nagging voices. I try to obey them both but it makes me all muddled in my mind. Oh, Hannah, please don't turn your back on me."

"Hannah will only keep facing forward if you clatter up the hillside and join us in our attempt to scale the third peak of Father's Mountain, isn't that right, Hannah?" Haggis taunted down. "So what do you say for this third and last time, cowardly Hamish? Remember, your reply will be do or die as far as Hannah is concerned. For me and my friends, you can remain a whining ninny for the rest of your life."

"I'm not a whining ninny, Hannah," yelled Hamish, despairingly. "It's just that with my multiplied vision I'd probably climb a peak that wasn't there if

I joined you in the mountains. Anyway, though it's a perfect morning I'm certain we're in for a snowstorm later."

The gang on the hillside groaned with delight to hear such a silly lie. Trying to out-groan each other, some of them slipped from their rocky boulders to end up on their backs, hooves in the air. But then young mountain goats often overdo their disbelief and bruise themselves.

"Well, gang," said Haggis briskly, "I think I proved my point days ago. We're wasting precious climbing time trying to put a bit of backbone into Hamish. Do we agree that we should leave him dreaming in his heathery bed on the safe valley floor, and get on with the business we goats were built for? Namely, clattering up dangerous mountains? So, Hannah, are you ready to tell Hamish that his latest lie is the straw that broke the goat's back?"

"Almost, Haggis," cried a distraught Hannah. "I an itching to tell Hamish to go and whistle after his latest illness excuse. I am dying to tell him things that will hurt him and me equally cruelly. In fact I am on the point of telling him that he can go and stew in his own thin Highland broth."

"But aren't you going to ask me about my new hobby, Hannah?" shouted the frantic Hamish up the hillside, the pressure of so many voices having a go at him, threatening to at last turn him completely mad. "Please say that you will be intrigued to learn about what I plan to do until my eye-sight problem clears up. You were always interested before."

"Interests can wane, Hamish," called Hannah, tears welling into her mauve eyes as she tossed her wispy beard, angrily. "And I'm beginning to feel that my true interests lie with brave Haggis and the gang."

"Well, I would be intrigued to hear about your new hobby, Hamish," shouted Haggis, grinning down the hillside. "So what do you plan to astound us with today?"

"Only the bravest hobby of all," yelled back the defiant Hamish, shuddering even as he spoke the lie. "Having mastered pot-holing, and having set an unbreakable record as a long-distance swimmer and monster-basher, I today intend to clatter over to the next mountain and place my front hooves over the boundary line that Huge Hughie guards so fiercely. Then I plan to shout as loudly as I can, 'how's that for trespassing, ugly Huge Hughie?' And when he bellows 'get off my property or face the consequences' I will coolly refuse and challenge him to a butting-contest. That is my new hobby. And, me being a pretty good butter, I will probably butt him all over the place."

The gang of young goats on the hillside gasped. Had they heard right? Had they actually heard cowardly Hamish say that he planned to lock horns with Huge

Hughie for a hobby? For the legend went that Huge Hughie's cave was stacked with the whitening bones of goats who had dared to cross his boundary line. Quivering with excitement they stared through round eyes at Haggis, who sensibly, was as afraid of Huge Hughie as any goat in the Highlands. But Haggis knew a lie when he heard one, however terrifying. He was not at all thrown by Hamish's suicidal boast.

"Come now Hamish," he giggled. "Huge Hughie over the next mountain would eat you alive as a hobby of his own. Anyway, why should a goat prefer being savaged by Huge Hughie when he could be kicking up fresh snow on the third peak of Father's Mountain? So, what do you think about Hamish's latest mad hobby, Hannah?"

"I must admit it's just too gallant to be true, especially for Hamish, Haggis," confessed Hannah, broken-heartedly. "This time, Hamish's lies have out-

grown even him. For such a hobby would prove to be the greatest folly in the history of Highland goatdom. For only a goat named Hercules could take on Huge Hughie and live to tell the tale. Certainly not Hamish who only tells tales to live. Sadly, Haggis, I am forced to admit that Hamish's latest hobby would be a grave act of folly, if true."

"Though never a charming and flashy act of folly, Hannah?" called Hamish anxiously. "I want you to understand that it's only something to pass away the time until my eye-sight improves enough for me to lead you all up Father's Mountain."

"Well, we think your new hobby is waffle, Hamish," yelled Haggis down the hillside. "I am willing to bet that the moment we set off to climb the third peak of Father's Mountain you will snuggle down on your heathery bed and dream about rescuing the likes of beautiful 'Hannah' from the clutches of villains that exist only in your mixed-up mind. Oh, come on gang, let us clatter upwards towards the third peak of Father's Mountain and breathe the heady air there. For the air down here is getting stale. Let's leave the pathetic Hamish to his world of dreams where we have no place, and have never wanted one."

With that he spun around on his private rock and, jumping down, clattered off up the hillside, the gang as loyal as ever clattering in his wake. Only Hannah spared a last brief moment for Hamish who was picking himself up from his sore nose and crumpled beard after yet another phoney fall over another hummock of turf.

"Poor Hamish," she whispered down the hillside, her wispy beard sadly wagging to and fro. "And still you stubbornly lie. How could you? And all the faith I had in you once. Now I know that no matter how glorious the climbing morning you will always find some excuse for not coming with us. Well, Hamish, I am going now. And when I return from the high mountains I doubt if I'll want to speak to you ever again," and with those bitter words she turned and left.

CHAPTER SIX

Hamish, crippled by the nagging voices in his head, his own lies, and Hannah's loss of faith in him, curled himself up on his heathery bed on the safe valley floor and tried to bury his sorrow in sleep. But he couldn't sleep. For even in his cowardly soul there still remained a spark of self respect. And from that near-empty well, Hamish summoned it forth.

"I swear that this new hobby will not

find me wanting," he cried at the sky where a brave lark buffeted his way to Heaven's Gate. "I swear, I will cross over to the next mountain and tussle it out with Huge Hughie, if only to die, if only to make Hannah see that deep-down I was amongst the bravest of the brave."

"I think I've heard that song before, son," murmured his father in his right ear. "For pluck was never in the saying, but in the doing. But I do hope I've heard right, for you are long overdue for a bit of swaggering about. And Huge Hughie isn't so very big when confronted head-on."

"But what if our Hamish swaggers straight on to Huge Hughie's sharp horns?" hissed the voice of Hamish's dead mother into her son's left ear. "What if he ends up a small pile of whitening bones in that bully's cave? No, Hamish lad, leave all that show-off stuff to the likes of Haggis who will never make old bones, and will be extremely

late for his tea one of these days."

Reeling from their struggle for his soul, Hamish closed tight his pink eyes and willed sleep to come. And it did, though accompanied by yet another nightmare . . .

. . . through the blinding snowstorm Hamish with his double vision could just make out the two Hannahs crying with pain as the four savage horns of the two Huge Hughies sought to finish their deadly work.

"Help me, Hamish," screamed Hannah. "Cross over Huge Hughie's boundary line and try to save my life. For I'm all alone and about to die for crossing the bully's boundary line by accident. And yet I realise that your skin is just as important as mine, Hamish. So if you would rather flee and save yourself I will understand. I won't hold it against you."

"Thanks for being concerned about my precious skin, Hannah," yelled

Hamish, spitting out lumps of blizzard. "I will take up your kind offer. Only, what with the violence of the snowstorm and what with my double vision seeing two Huge Hughies, I don't think I'd be much use to you."

Then, turning to flee, Hamish was barged by an enormous snowball rushing past him, heading for Huge Hughie's boundary line. It was Haggis.

"Out of the way, you cowardly wally," snarled Haggis, hurling Hamish aside into the snow. Then without pausing another second, Haggis hurled himself at Hannah's tormentor, the force of his charge sending the much bigger goat reeling back in surprise, his sharp and famous horns crumpling and shattering to pieces before the savage impact of Haggis's determination.

Crouched for safety on the other side of the boundary line, Hamish miserably heard the cheers ring out as Haggis came skidding back over the boundary line sledging the limp and frozen form of Hannah behind him. After seeing that Hannah was still alive, the gang of goats promptly led off their hero and heroine for a slap-up tea and a sing-song in celebration of the humbling of Huge Hughie. Hamish, still seeing twice the number of goats a goat normally should, was ignored and left alone with his double vision and his single, bitter loneliness.

With a start Hamish awoke from his snowy nightmare just in time to see the sun setting warmly red behind the mountains. Shifting his bleary gaze he noted that his old neighbour the lark was back in his new nest, his beady eyes watching the young goat warily. But the bird had nothing to fear from Hamish who was too wrapped up in his humiliation to harm a nest of innocent chicks. Anyway, he loved and admired the larks, though he'd never say.

"Well, Hamish, as a coward you've certainly earned full marks this time," grated the voice of his dead father in his right ear. "Oh if only I had bred a son like Haggis instead of a wash-out called Hamish."

"At least my Hamish will not end up as a small pile of whitening bones in Huge Hughie's cave," countered mother in Hamish's left. "At least my Hamish had the sense to realise that it's better to be a shy coward than a flashy hero who won't live long. I'm thinking of that charming Haggis who is, I'm certain, living on borrowed time as far as tea-time is concerned."

But she was wrong again. For just at that moment Haggis came sauntering down from the mountains, the gang in his wake, and Hannah too. Haggis could hardly contain his triumph.

"Hey, Hamish," he yelled down the hillside. "Guess who's tucked the third peak of Father's Mountain under his

Hamish

belt? Of course, being a gallant goat I allowed Hannah the honour of being the first to break the crisp snow there. But it was I who figured out the best route to the summit. So how went your tussle to the death with Huge Hughie? I must say you don't look very bruised to me. But then why should you appear wounded when you haven't stirred from your heathery bed all day? What do you say, Hannah?"

"I'm afraid I must agree with you, Haggis," cried Hannah, a tear in her mauve eye. "Hamish certainly doesn't look as though he's tangled with Huge Hughie and come off either first or second best. But then, everyone I admire always falls short of my faith in them, isn't that correct, Hamish?"

"You are correct as always, Hannah," shouted Hamish, completely missing the point. But at least Hannah had spoken to him, he sighed with relief. Then came the lies. "Of course, Hannah, Haggis is not correct at all. In fact I did cross over Huge Hughie's boundary line and thrash him to within an inch of his life. But then as you know, Hannah, I like to succeed in every new hobby I take up."

"You actually came to grips with Huge Hughie?" mocked Haggis. "I can't imagine how you did that, what with your double vision problem, and all in a blinding snowstorm too. So what happened to your predicted snowstorm? For the gang will tell you that the only snow we ploughed through on Father's Mountain was lying settled on the third peak. Oh, Hamish, mighty destroyer of Huge Hughie, when are you going to give up your hobbies that are nothing but dreams and come climbing in the mountains as a true goat should?"

"You wait until I'm truly fit, then I'll show you, Haggis," bellowed Hamish up the hill side. "Unless I should develop another illness in the meantime, of course. I can hardly be fit if I'm ill, can I, Hannah?"

"Oh, come on gang," said Haggis, disgusted. "Why do we waste time on the lying dreamer? Anyway, I'm dying for my tea, and it's fresh brambles and stinging nettles tonight, lovely grub." And off he clattered at full tilt for home, the ravenous gang at full tilt on his heels. Only Hannah was prepared to let tea-time wait awhile. For though she had given up on Hamish, her heart was as good as gold, ever siding with the despised underdog.

"So, what are you doing for the rest of your life, Hamish?" she called down, pity in her tone. "For I think it's going to take an awful lot of dreams to last you through to the end of it. And to think that at one time my own dreams seemed to be so closely linked with yours. But I must also dash off home for my tea, for my little brother has the annoying habit of finishing his own and starting on mine if I'm more than a few seconds late. So goodbye, Hamish, perhaps on the next perfect climbing morning I will nod the time of day at you, for I will certainly be unable to speak."

And off she dashed in floods of tears leaving Hamish in floods of his own.

CHAPTER SEVEN

For a long time that night Hamish thought seriously about doing away with himself. His father in his right ear thought it a brilliant idea, his mother in his left thought it was plain stupid and dangerous. But how to commit suicide, that was the problem for a small mountain goat who had reached the end of his tether. He could throw himself down a deep pot-hole, but the thought of all those little, blind, snapping crabs nipping at his dead beard gave Hamish the shudders. Perhaps he could drown himself in the Loch, but the image of being dragged to the bottom to fill the monster's larder caused his stomach to turn to water. How about if he ran away and died of starvation and loneliness over the next mountain? But the idea of his thin body being stomped on and mangled by Huge Hughie caused Hamish to think again. Of course, there was always the obvious way. Living among the mountains as he did he could throw himself off a high peak, but Hamish hated heights with every fibre of his small being, so that was out. So, he pondered tearfully, how could he end his life without hurting himself?

Suddenly, in his ears, above the bickering of his parents, Hamish heard the sweetest music. Soft and low at first, it soon filled the night with glorious song. The melody was picked up by another voice, this one hovering throatily around the middle notes. Then a third voice joined in harmony. Simple and fluting, it claimed the high range, to weave all those haunting sounds into pictures. The songsters were the three lark chicks who lived with their parents, thankfully not too near to the small, mad goat. Tired of being protected from the world, they were fretting to shrug off the influence of their living parents, anxious to soar freely into the blue sky and praise

God for themselves. And their yearnings struck a chord in the heart of a small mountain goat called Hamish. For he himself had always lived under the wings of his dominant parents. As the lovely song of the lark chicks died away, so Hamish fell into a deep and untroubled sleep, his dreams filled with hope and an excited longing to at last strike out in life on his own, to begin a new. And that magical night gave way to a glorious morning full of fresh horizons for four determined young hearts.

CHAPTER EIGHT

"Hamish, oh Hamish, it's another perfect climbing day, will you dare to come and join us?" The challenge drifted down the hillside and into the waiting ears of a small mountain goat.

Never before had Hamish been glad to hear that mocking voice. Jumping eagerly from his heathery bed he gazed expectantly up the hillside where the gang were jostling for the most unsafe boulders to balance on. Early that morning Hamish had watched the three lark chicks struggle from their nest and, encouraged by their parents, soar into the blue sky, to have a crack at God and His Heaven for themselves. Now it was his turn to ring the changes, thought Hamish, excitedly. Ignoring the voice of his dead mother who was so against it, and also the spirit of his father who was urging him, "for once in your life be flash and swank a bit", Hamish answered Haggis's challenge with every fibre of his small being. There was no swank, no flash in his reply . . . just confidence . . .

"A perfect climbing morning indeed, Haggis," he shouted up the hillside. "In fact the ideal morning for me to clatter up the hillside and show you and the gang and Hannah some real climbing. Hang on a second while I flex my hooves in readiness."

Haggis was dumbstruck. So was the gang. So was Hannah. In fact they were all so shocked by Hamish's sudden fitness that some of them fell from their boulders and stubbed their wispily-bearded chins on the hard slope of the hillside again. Regaining their feet they began to discuss with awe Hamish's latest, most absurd of lies, so unbelievable as to put all his others to shame. Only the old lark who was having a rest from Heaven that day knew that Hamish wasn't lying this time. He now felt as proud of his old neighbour as he did of his sky-bound singing chicks. In the meantime Hamish was trying to control his enthusiasm for his new-found courage and vigour. But it was hard, for young mountain goats are hopeless at hiding their feelings when they want the whole world to share them. However, Haggis was not in a sharing mood.

"What, *you* climb Father's Mountain with all your ailments?" he jeered. "Come off it, Hamish. So what is the new illness you plan to spring on us? For since when were you ever willing to climb without an excuse intruding? What do you say, Hannah?"

"I'd like to think that Hamish feels as fit as he says," grieved Hannah. "But I cannot believe in him any more. Regretfully I think that Hamish is leading us up the garden path again with his brave new talk. I have the sinking feeling that he is leading up to telling us about another unlikely hobby that will perfectly suit some new damage to his body. Am I right, Hamish?"

"For the first time in your life you are wrong, Hannah," shouted a jubilant Hamish up the hillside. "For in fact I've given up hobbies to take up climbing mountains full-time. Please believe me, Hannah, for I am truly a new goat, thanks to three angelic voices and the effect they had on me."

"Which must be Hamish's new hobby," said Haggis, wisely shaking his wispy beard. "If he's been listening to angelic voices it can only mean that he is delving deeply into religion. Which also means that he's gone completely haywire. Oh, come on gang, let's leave the coward to his psalm-singing, for we have the fourth and final peak of Father's Mountain to conquer before tea-time tonight." So saying, he jumped from his personal rock and lead the way up the hillside, the gang, all shaking their youthful beards in disapproval of Hamish's new hobby, clattering along behind. Only Hannah, whose heart was still as pure as gold, remained behind for a moment.

"Why won't the gang believe me, Hannah?" shouted Hamish, miserably. "Now, just when I've changed and become my own goat, they still reject me. Surely you believe I've reformed, Hannah?"

"If only I *could* believe you, Hamish," wept Hannah. "But after your past behaviour, I can't. The new Hamish you want me to trust seems to be the old one talking like some sad Saint. But I can't linger longer, Hamish. The gang has awarded me the honour of setting the first hoof on the final peak of your father's mountain. I just hope I'm brave enough to do what you fear so much. So, goodbye for ever, my beloved but lost Hamish. May you enjoy your new hobby being a Saint. And if I return from the mountains I won't greet you as an old friend. For I couldn't bear it if you

preached at me and called me wicked
for loving madcap climbing adventures.
But I'll miss you, Hamish, I truly
will . . ."

Then she too had gone a–clattering up
the hillside.

Rejected and dejected, Hamish
slumped in his heathery bed on the safe
valley floor. Not even the kindly "never
mind" clucking of the lark parents could
lift him from despair.

"As a cowardly worm you've turned
too late, son," sighed his father in his
right ear. "Because of your lies you only
have larks for friends. You should have
been larking and swaggering about on
your own account, many tall stories ago.
Now even Hannah despises you."

"At least Hamish hasn't fallen from a
high peak, have you, son?" hissed mother
in his left. "Anyway, I'm proud of you
becoming a preacher. At least preachers
are always the first goats to settle down to
tea when a quiet day is almost done."

But Hamish no longer cared what his dead parents shouted in his opposite ears. He just wanted to escape his returned misery. Turning over in his grassy bed he was just about to fall asleep, to dream his woes away when he heard the clattering of hooves on rock above him. Lifting his head Hamish saw one of the gang scrambling down the hillside all out of breath.

"Hamish, oh Hamish," the small goat gasped down the hillside. "Hannah is trapped on the fourth and final peak of Father's Mountain. Me and the gang are not brave enough to rescue her, and Haggis seems reluctant to try. So I beg you, Hamish, become again what you once were, the best young climber in the Highlands, and race up the mountain to rescue her before she falls to her death."

"Clatter back up there as fast as you can and tell Hannah to hang on," yelled Hamish, every fibre of his body tingling with grit. For though he feared and hated

Father's Mountain, his love for Hannah was much much stronger. "Tell her that she will never fall from Father's Mountain as long as there is breath in Hamish's body, plus strong, fit hooves beneath him."

CHAPTER NINE

Fighting his fear every inch of the way, Hamish began the long clatter up the mountain that had claimed the life of his father. The climb cost him much, for he was not only fighting the mountain but also his parents who battled to control his mind. His dread and the weather combined against him, making his upwards dash a trial that no young goat should ever have to face. Arriving on the first peak, all his lies came flooding back to torment him.

"Go back down and lie on your heathery bed, Hamish," shrieked his mother in his left ear above the buffeting of the wind. "Why attempt to be a flashy show-off with your life on the line, especially when that handicapped hoof of yours must be killing you?"

"Take no notice, son, brave the storm and the pain from your hoof," urged the voice of his dead father. "Set your eyes upwards, for only there will you save yourself and that which you love."

But Hamish no longer needed advice. He knew what he must do, for deep-down he had always been amongst the bravest of the brave. Battling the storm and the agony from his handicapped hoof, panting he arrived on the second peak of Father's Mountain. On that new summit fresh conditions awaited to plague him. Gulping down huge lungfuls of air he tried to control the spinning of his head that suddenly felt as heavy as a turnip. Meanwhile, all around him raged a hurricane. "Hamish, Hamish, don't lose your head over something that isn't worth it,' screamed his mother in his left ear. "Go back down the valley where your head will feel as light as a lettuce again. Is this Hannah worth flashily braving a hurricane for?"

"You've beaten the storm and your crock hoof, son," yelled his father above the whirling hurricane. "Press on upwards, son, for if you turn back now you'll be pressing flowers and spotting chaffinches for the rest of your cowardly life."

Taking no notice of them both, Hamish grimly pointed his wispy beard upwards, his determined pink eyes taking in the needle-sharp peak that seemed to beckon, "come and try me, silly little goat." Instantly his hooves were clattering upwards again, towards his destiny. As he neared, so his head felt lighter, the hurricane that he had forged through finally dying away. And suddenly, weary though still determined, he clattered on to the third peak of Father's Mountain. The terrible blizzard sleeting down, the trouble he had focussing his double vision eyes, all combined with his tiredness, sapping his will to go on.

"Now do you see what I mean, Hamish?" appealed his mother in his left ear. "No goat in the Highlands would want to be up here when they could be down in the valley, lying on a nice heathery bed. I implore you, Hamish, don't be like your father and die flashily, with no tea-time to look forward to."

"Three peaks down, and one to go, son," bawled his father in his right ear. "Wipe your eyes clear of snow and double-vision and gaze steadfastly upwards. For you're nearly there and will make it if you are a son of mine."

Twitching his ears shut against the blizzard and his parents, Hamish forged upwards towards that last remaining peak. And suddenly, after much exertion, he was there. As he clattered on to that peak that he had for so long feared to even think about, so the weather fell calm, and the blue sky was filled with sunshine. But his mission was much more important. Gazing around, he soon spied what he sought. He also heard.

"Haggis . . . gang . . . anyone . . . please help me, for I'm afraid that if I move a muscle I will fall to the valley below," cried Hannah. Then, praying for the impossible, "Hamish, oh dreaming, cowardly Hamish, if only you were here to realise the faith I once had in you. For then you would race up Father's Mountain and rescue me, for Haggis surely won't." And then through frantic eyes she saw the actual, impossible: "Hamish," she screamed. "Oh, Hamish."

But Hamish had no time for soppy stuff at the moment. Brushing aside the gang and the shame-faced Haggis, he scrutinized the perilous situation Hannah was in. She was perched on a crag, her four hooves trying to find secure footing on rock enough for only one hoof. Behind her, the narrow ledge that she had so confidently clattered along to gain her perch, had unexpectedly crumbled away. Now there was no way back or

down for her, save for a plummeting fall
into the valley below. Then Hamish
spoke. Words of such cool courage that
the gang gasped, noting how the
bragging Haggis remained silent.

"Think of me as a bridge to safety,
Hannah," Hamish called, "for that's
what my body is about to become. I plan
to become a narrow bridge that is no
longer there. I intend to anchor my rear
hooves in this rock, and my fore-hooves
on the rock I am standing on. Then,
when I shout 'clatter over me, Hannah',
I will grit my teeth and hang on so tight
that you will be able to run over me
to safety. Are you ready, Hannah, for
I am?"

"Grip and hang on tight, my bravest of
the brave," cried Hannah, leaping from
her terrible perch and clattering across
the goat-made bridge that was the
groaning body of her beloved Hamish.
"And I take back all my awful words that
I spat at you when you were dreaming

on your heathery bed, safe on the valley floor. For I am saved, and you, my cowardly Hamish, rescued me."

Which was one in the eye for Haggis who was now skulking about the rocks like the real coward he was. It was also one in the many eyes of the gang who had got their heroes wrong, now anxious to butter up their new hero, Hamish. And so they all wended their way back down Father's Mountain, the happy rescuer and the rescued, the sullen Haggis and the gleeful gang. But as they clattered to where the safe valley met the hillside, so all enmities dispersed, and they became a happy gang of mountain goats again, with Hamish the new and rightful leader, of course. And they were all quite early for tea. And Hamish was invited round to share so many tea-times that his belly got quite fat. But then, that is the price you pay for being an enormously popular hero who is never flashy . . . nor a show off . . . nor . . . well, who is just himself. Not only brave, Hamish was merciful. He refused to take tea with anyone unless Haggis was also invited. For young mountain goats are extremely forgiving, even to their bitterest enemies . . .

And to end a beautiful day the three young lark chicks spiralled down from their crack at Heaven, having not quite achieved it, but hoping to soon, God bless . . .

Hodder's July Story Book

The Silkie

Sandra Ann Horn

Wee Jeannie doesn't realise how lonely she is until she
falls in love with a Silkie from deep under the sea.
Casting off his sealskin he comes to shore in human
form - but only under a full moon.

Jeannie wishes he would stay forever. But only by
trickery and magic is this possible, and by risking the
life of the person she loves most in the world ...

A beautiful story about love and friendship.

HODDER'S YEAR OF STORIES
for the NATIONAL YEAR OF READING

Why not collect all twelve Story Books in *Hodder's Year of Stories?*

ORDER FORM

Please select your Year of Reading Story Books from the previous page

---

All Hodder Children's books are available at your local bookshop or newsagent, or can be ordered direct from the publisher. Just tick the titles you want and fill in the form below. Prices and availability subject to change without notice.

Hodder Children's Books, Cash Sales Department, Bookpoint, 39 Milton Park, Abingdon, OXON, OX14 4TD, UK. If you have a credit card you may order by telephone - (01235) 831700.

Please enclose a cheque or postal order made payable to Bookpoint Ltd to the value of the cover price and allow the following for postage and packing:
UK & BFPO - £1.00 for the first book, 50p for the second book, and 30p for each additional book ordered up to a maximum charge of £3.00.
OVERSEAS & EIRE - £2.00 for the first book, £1.00 for the second book, and 50p for each additional book.

Name...

Address ....

....

....

If you would prefer to pay by credit card, please complete:
Please debit my Visa/Access/Diner's Card/American Express (delete as applicable) card no.

Signature...
Expiry Date..